Help!

My

pony's

gone

potty

THE INTERNET VET

Help!
My
pony's
gone
potty

Tony De Saulles

■SCHOLASTIC

For Alice and Jasper

With thanks to horse experts Jackie May and Barry Upton

Many thanks to Pete Wedderburn of the Brayvet Animal Hospital for
his expert comments on the text of all the Internet Vet books

Scholastic Children's Books,
Commonwealth House, 1-19 New Oxford Street,
London WC1A 1NU, UK

A division of Scholastic Ltd
London ~ New York ~ Toronto ~ Sydney ~ Auckland
Mexico City ~ New Delhi ~ Hong Kong

Published in the UK by Scholastic Ltd, 2003

Printed and bound by Nørhaven Paperback A/S, Denmark

2 4 6 8 10 9 7 5 3 1

Contents

Front Page Moos   7

The Grumpy Chicken   15

Mr McMisery   24

Paddocks and Padlocks   43

It's the Pits!   70

Identity Crisis   90

Heroes!   105

Front Page Moos

Our Internet Vet website was doing well. Hardly surprising – we were offering BRILLIANT FREE PET ADVICE! Pet lovers from all around the world were contacting us. And Dad was making money, too. Pet product companies were dead keen to advertise on our site. It was like a shop window that everyone in the world could see into. Parrot poop-catchers, anti-fart tablets for dogs, leashes for lizards and snacks for snakes – all could be purchased with the click of a button!

But the bit I liked best was helping people with their pet problems. You wouldn't believe some of the things we've had to sort out. Just take a look at our Internet Vet Home Page…

IS YOUR CAT DEEPLY STRESSED?

AND YOUR DOG HAVING FITS?

QUEASY KITTENS?
POORLY PUPPIES?
GET ON–LINE AND. . .

 Email your pet problems to me, Doug Kennel, The Internet Vet

 Post messages and photos on the Internet Pet Board

 Advertise your weird and wonderful pet products and remember:

IF YOUR PET'S UPSET CALL THE INTERNET VET!

And it wasn't just the money that Dad was enjoying. He was becoming a sort of celebrity! Any chance to get on local radio or in the news and Dad was up for it. Sad, really. In fact, sad and TOTALLY EMBARRASSING! A little girl walked up to him in the supermarket last week. "Hello, Internet Vet man!" she squeaked. Dad was *so* chuffed. Grinning like an idiot, he insisted on autographing her carrier bag. Ugh!

Zak and I thought we might have to remind him that starting the website was *our* idea, not his. I mean, yes, he might be the "vet" bit of the Internet Vet website but he couldn't run it without Zak's computer knowledge or my brilliant drawings.

As it turned out, we didn't need to remind Dad of anything. Something happened that brought him down to earth with a very loud bump, or should I say, CRACK! Getting a mention in the local newspaper, he found out, wasn't *always* a pleasant experience.

The Prestbury Post

INTERNET VET GETS ARM STUCK IN COW!

INTERNET VET, DOUG KENNEL, IS RECOVERING IN HOSPITAL THIS MORNING AFTER A FREAKY FARMYARD ACCIDENT.

~

Local dairy farmer, Chris Milcowski, had called Mr Kennel when his cow started having calving problems.

"It's quite normal for a vet to feel inside a cow in this sort of trouble," Mr Milcowski explained. "Once he knows the position of the unborn calf, he can move it around to make the birth easier. I can usually do it myself, but this was a tricky one."

And as it turned out, it wasn't just tricky for the cow.

Chris Milcowski

"All was going well," the farmer told us. "I'd supplied some soapy water for Mr Kennel and he started to have a feel inside Daisy.

"Suddenly, Daisy moved to one side and caught Mr Kennel off balance. The combination of this, and the unfortunate vet slipping on a cowpat, twisted him into a painful position. He seemed rather upset. Distressed, you might say.
"'Argh, my arm!' he screamed.
"'Jumpin' jellyfish, I think I've broken it!'

"At least I think that's what he said. Anyway, he wasn't too enthusiastic about the help I was offering him.
"'Get away, don't touch me! Ughhhh ... call an ambulance, QUICK!' he wailed.
"I used his mobile to call for help and also for another vet.

After all, it wasn't just Mr Kennel who had problems. What about poor old Daisy?"

Indeed, both vet and cow were in a bad way. However, the situation was soon under control with Doug Kennel rushed to casualty and another vet on site to take over.

Relief vet Matt Smuggins picks up the story.

M. SMUGGINS

"I'm not sure how things had got into such a mess, but it was important to sort the situation out quickly. The cow was clearly distressed and it took all my professional expertise to get things under control.

"I don't think Doug visits many farms these days. He seems to spend most of his time zapping off emails to the other side of the world. Perhaps his practical veterinary skills are getting rusty while he's sitting at his computer."

"THINGS IN A MESS?" Dad spluttered into his cornflakes. "SKILLS GETTING RUSTY? The cheek of the man. If it wasn't for him opening his new surgery down the road, I wouldn't have needed to start the website in the first place!"

We nodded obediently as he waved the paper in the air and winced. The bad publicity seemed to be hurting Dad as much as his broken arm. Zak tried to cheer him up. "Smuggins is jealous of your success," he said.

"Yeah!" I agreed. "He knows you're one of the best vets around.

He's just trying to give you a bad name so he can steal more of your customers."

It was the truth but there was no way to prove it. Slurping down his tea, Dad shuffled off to work with a face like a bulldog sucking a wasp.

But Dad's gloom didn't last for ever. Something happened that offered him a chance to snap out of his depression and put things right.

It all started with three odd emails from a boy called Joe…

The Grumpy Chicken

To: The Internet Vet
From: Joe Appleyard
Place: Isle of Jigg, Scotland

Dear Internet Vet

I've got trouble with one of my chickens –
hope you can help. The daft bird's turned
grumpy and refuses to come out of the
nesting box. This means the other hens can't
get in, so they've been laying their eggs
elsewhere.

I have to search all over the place for them
and it's driving me nuts! What should I do?

Joe

This was the first of the odd emails and, after jotting down some notes, Dad asked Zak to type a reply. I'm not sure if Dad was *really* as busy as he claimed. I think perhaps the *"arm stuck in cow"* incident was still getting him down. Anyway, I hadn't finished my end-of-term exams, so *I* couldn't help. Zak had done all of his and got A+'s in everything (except art, of course). But before he'd had a chance to mail Joe back, another plea for help came through.

To: The Internet Vet
From: Joe Appleyard
Place: Isle of Jigg, Scotland

Dear Internet Vet

Things are getting worse. Now my blimin' cow, Decibelle, has kicked the bucket!

I don't mean she's dead; I mean she's as grumpy as the chicken. Just as I finish milking her, she moos and kicks the bucket over.

What's wrong with her?

Joe

Then the same thing happened again. Before Zak could type up Dad's notes, a third email arrived.

To: The Internet Vet
From: Joe Appleyard
Place: Isle of Jigg, Scotland

Dear Internet Vet

Help! Now the geese are behaving like the chicken and the cow. When I try to put them away in their house each evening, they hiss and spit at me. Sometimes they even attack me – they're evil!

I don't get it. Even my sister's pony's gone potty. What *is* going on?

Joe

I called into the office to see what Zak was up to. (I know I should have been revising but I needed a break.)

"S'pose I'd better get typing," he mumbled, shuffling Dad's notes into a pile. "This boy sounds a bit stressed, doesn't he?"

Stressed? Is that all Zak had noticed? Didn't he find it odd that somebody with so many animals could be so hopeless at looking after them?

"Aren't you the tiniest bit interested?" I asked. "Grumpy chickens? Potty ponies? Something weird's going on here and you've got to find out what it is!"

"Why? He's asked some questions, I'm sending the answers!" Zak replied. Honestly, he might have a brain the size of a small planet but he's got absolutely no imagination.

"Well, let me add something to the end of your email," I said.

He shrugged his shoulders. "Sure."

THE INTERNET VET

To: Joe Appleyard
From: Zak Kennel

Hi Joe

My dad (The Internet Vet) asked me to send you this info.

Your chicken's not grumpy – she's broody. She wants to have babies and she's determined to sit stubbornly on her eggs until they hatch. Problem is, unless you've got a cockerel (a male chicken) living with the hens, her eggs won't be fertile.

NO COCKEREL, NO CHICKS!

In other words, she'll be wasting her time!

You've got two choices. The best thing would be to give her some fertile eggs to sit on. But you'll need to put her in a nesting box of her own so the other birds don't bother her. If you want to stop her being broody, you'll need to make her uncomfortable. Put her in a draughty cage – it'll make her so uncomfortable that a few days' confinement will persuade her to stop being broody.

Your cow's not grumpy, either. She's probably got sore udders and finds it painful when you're milking her. Perhaps you're not doing it properly. Take a look at the pics below, they might help.

THE PROPER WAY TO MILK A COW!

Sit on a short stool with the bucket gripped firmly between your knees. Make sure your cow has something nice to eat before you start milking!

SQUIRT!

MUNCH!

MILK!

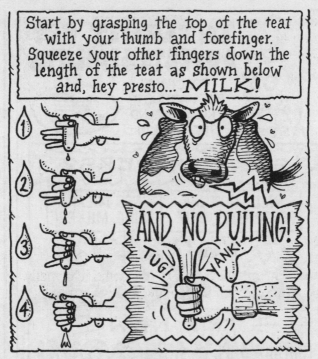

And get some udder cream! She'll be a different animal once it's soothed and healed her sore bits. The advertisement at the end of this email will put you in the picture.

As for your geese: yes, they can be a bit noisy but that's why people sometimes keep them instead of guard dogs. Dad reckons you're trying to put them in their house too early in the evening. Wait until it's almost dark, then they'll waddle to bed, no problem.

Anyway, here's the udder cream advert I mentioned.

INTERNET VET ADVERTISEMENTS

PURCHASE PET PRODUCTS FROM AROUND THE WORLD!

SORE UDDERS?

WELL NOT ME PERSONALLY, BUT... | **WE DREAD BEING MILKED!**

TRY NEW

UDDERLY SMOOVE!

Apply before milking. The medicated formula will heal and soothe sore udders, reducing pain and relaxing your milkers. It'll soothe and heal your hands, too!

UDDERLY SMOOVE!

NOW THE COWS ARE SO HAPPY... | **WE GAVE HIM A PAT ON THE HEAD!**

22

Good luck

Zak

PS My sister, Beth, was interested to hear about your sister's pony so she's added a message below.

Hi, I'm Beth. Sorry for being nosy but what's wrong with your sister's pony? Is there anything we can do to help?

Of course I wasn't sorry for being nosy at all, I just wanted to find out what was going on! And when I did, I was glad I'd stuck my nose in...

Mr McMisery

The exams were over and the holidays had started. Time to relax, have loads of lie-ins and meet up with my mates in town. Yeah, as if!

Dad was still operating (not literally!) with only one arm and I was needed more than ever. Any treatment requiring both of Dad's arms had to be referred to another vet. That's right: Matt Smuggins! Poor Dad, it was a disaster. But looking down at his plastered arm, I couldn't help smiling. Friends had insisted on signing the cast. It was covered in terrible corny cow jokes. The only person who didn't seem to find it funny was Dad.

We were treating a hamster with a gunged-up eye. While I held it, Dad set about cleaning up the little chap with his good hand. It didn't take long.

The morning shift was over so I popped the hamster back in his cage (he carried on cleaning himself as if not satisfied with our efforts) and strolled into the office.

Just when I was starting to think we'd never hear from the Isle of Jigg again, an email came through from Alice Appleyard, Joe's sister.

To: Beth Kennel and
The Internet Vet
From: Alice Appleyard
Place: Isle of Jigg, Scotland

HELP!

Dear Beth

Yes, I hope you can help! I think my pony, Lotty Trotter, is going mad. She walks round in circles all day long and keeps kicking the stable door.

I think *I* might go potty if she carries on like this!

Any idea what's wrong?

Alice Appleyard

Not much to go on, was it? I showed the email to Zak but he said he'd already helped the other kid and the pony problem was up to me. I'd ask Dad, of course, but before we could help we needed more info. I sent a brief reply.

From: Beth Kennel

Hi Alice

We'd love to help but we need more details.

How long have you had Lotty? Has she always been like this?

I don't mean to be rude, but you and your brother seem to have lots of animals and no idea how to look after them. How come?

Best wishes

Beth

"That's a bit strong!" Zak said when he saw my email.

"Yes, well, sometimes you've got to be blunt to get to the bottom of things," I replied. And though I say so myself, it did the trick. Another email came through that evening and this one explained everything!

To: Beth Kennel
From: Alice Appleyard
Place: Isle of Jigg, Scotland

HELP!

Hello Beth

Thanks for offering to help. Sorry about the last email – it's just that Lotty Trotter's not quite the pony I hoped she'd be and I'm *so* disappointed!

I had a look at Joe's emails and together with mine I can see that you must think it's us who are mad, not Lotty! I'll explain what's been going on.

Mum, Joe and I are looking after our Aunt Meg's smallholding (you know, like a little farm) on the Isle of Jigg while she visits her sister in Australia. Anyway, everything was great to start with. All we had to do was collect eggs, shut the chickens and geese away at night and keep an eye on the sheep. Duncan McDougal, the grumpy little handyman, did everything else (we call him Mr McMisery!). He's an ex-jockey and looks like he wishes we hadn't come to stay. We can't stand him! The only time he speaks to us is to have a moan. He's even banned us from certain parts of the smallholding – a barn in the middle of a big field. I mean, it's no big deal, we've got the whole island to explore. It's just the way the horrible man speaks to us. "Come 'ere yoo two! D'nay think of going into the field with the barn. I keep m'rat poison and pesticides in there and I'll 'av yer guts fer garters if yer go in there. It's strictly oot of boonds!" Charming, eh? And when he's not poisoning rats, he's either shooting pigeons or sending his ferrets down rabbit holes.

Then last week, something terrible happened. Duncan McDougal was struck down with a terrible illness. We were down in the kitchen when there was a loud thud above our heads. We rushed upstairs and knocked on McMisery's door but he wouldn't answer. So we knocked again and went in.

We found him unconscious on the floor – I THOUGHT HE WAS DEAD! I rushed off to find Mum. She always stays calm in a crisis and soon had everything under control. Duncan McDougal was rushed to hospital on the mainland and that's left *us* in charge of the smallholding!

Well, if I'm honest, Joe looks after most of the animals – I just take care of Lotty. She used to belong to Aunt Meg's daughter, but Suzy works on the mainland now. Honestly, I've been *so* looking forward to riding her. I'm mad about ponies but it costs a bomb to have lessons and I can't afford them. My grandmother treated me to a pony-trekking holiday last year, but I haven't ridden since. So, when Aunt Meg told me about Lotty and invited us to stay this summer, it sounded brilliant. But things haven't been as straightforward as I'd hoped.

I imagined galloping around the island, having horsey adventures. No such luck!

The thing is, Lotty hasn't been ridden for ages and she's acting funny. I told you about the walking in circles and kicking out but that's

not all. She's started rocking her head from side to side and chewing on her stable door. Sometimes, she clamps her mouth on the door

 and sucks air in through her teeth. It's rather creepy and I'm scared to ride her.

I must admit, things are a bit run-down here. Duncan McDougal was supposed to be fixing the fencing in the paddock but he hasn't got round to it.

But Lotty's stable is warm and dry and she's well fed, so what's the problem? Is there any way I can get Lotty to behave normally so I can ride her?

I'm so glad we found your website. There's no vet on Jigg and I need some advice!

Best wishes

Alice Appleyard

I printed out the email and took it through to Dad who was watching telly.

Squinting through his glasses, he read it with interest.

"Hmm, fascinating," he said. "I've got some info that's ideal for new pony owners. You can send that to Alice, for starters. But we'll need some advice on the pony's strange behaviour and that requires specialist knowledge."

"There's only one person to contact, then," I said. "Auntie Jackie."

"That's right. But she's usually really busy. Perhaps if I offer her a bit of a discount on the new advert we're doing for her; it might speed things up! I think Zak's finished doing the technical stuff for it. I'll email her in the morning."

The next day, after Dad had emailed Auntie Jackie, an email arrived for Zak.

To: Zak

Hi Zak

Thanks for your email. Sorry if my first email sounded a little stressed but things are going OK now!

Got the hang of milking Decibelle – I'd been pulling too hard and not squeezing like you're supposed to! Found some udder cream in a cupboard, too. The old girl's much happier now!

You were right about the geese. They're as good as gold if I wait till dusk.

And guess what? I've got some fertile eggs ... from Calum, the postman! He has a smallholding across the island – he's a friendly bloke. I told Calum about my lonely hen and he's given me a few eggs – FREE! She's out there now, sitting on them!

Calum's selling Mum one of his chickens, too. He even offered to show me how to kill and pluck it. Blimey, there's no way I'm doing that... I might watch, though!

Thanks,

Joe

PS You wouldn't believe some of the smells around here (or maybe you would, working at a vets!). The smell of cowpats is actually quite nice and chicken poo isn't too bad, either. But horse poo is almost as bad as doggy doos! Check out this chart...

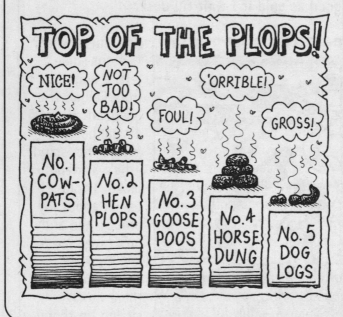

Zak was smiling. "He sounds like quite a laugh. I think I'll keep in touch."

"Because he's fascinated by animal dung?" I said. "How childish. Now get lost, 'cos I've got some proper pet info to send to Alice."

"Let me know when you've finished and I'll add a note for Joe," he replied.

"Oh all right, if you must," I said. "But it had better not be about poo!"

Zak was grinning again. "Oh no, it's about chickens. Honest!"

To: Alice
From: Beth

Hi Alice

Dad and I were very interested to read your email. No wonder you've been having so many animal problems! But we think the Lotty situation is more serious than grumpy chickens and miserable cows! I've asked for some advice from my Auntie who's a pony behaviour specialist. I'm sure she'll know what to do. In the mean time I've attached some info about getting to know your pony. It'll get you started, anyway, and I'll send the other info over as soon as it arrives.

Being pals with your pony!

Just started looking after a pony? Well, start as you mean to go on! A pony will only be happy, secure and well-behaved if its owner is relaxed, confident and in control. Read the following list carefully – it's the key to being pals with your pony...

Make sure you **DO** all these **DO'S!**

DO – praise your pony and give him lots of pats and strokes if he's behaving well.

DO – tell him off with a harsh tone when he's naughty. He'll soon learn what he is and isn't allowed to do.

DO – be consistent! Your pony will only understand you if you respond to him in the same way every time you're with him. Telling him off for something one day and not bothering the next will cause confusion and a breakdown in communication.

DO – spend lots of time with him. It's the only way to build a strong friendship with your pony.

And definitely **DON'T** do any of these **DON'TS**!

DON'T – hit your pony! Apart from being cruel it'll make him nervy and difficult to approach.

DON'T – spoil your pony with titbits all the time. He'll get in the habit of expecting a treat every time he sees you and may start misbehaving. It can even lead to biting!

DON'T keep changing his routine, it'll upset him! Try to do things at the same time and in the same way, each day.

DON'T – surprise or startle your pony.

Loud or sudden noises will make your pony nervous and might cause him to kick out. Be sure that he knows where you are, even if he can't see you.

Bye for now,

Beth

PS And I think Zak wants to add a message for your brother...

Hi Joe

Glad it's all going OK now.

You're right, Dad's surgery is a smelly place. We have to clear up all sorts of messes and some of them are *really* stinky!
Hearing about Calum the postman and his chickens reminded me of an advert we put together recently. Get a load of this!

INTERNET VET ADVERTISEMENTS

PURCHASE PET PRODUCTS FROM AROUND THE WORLD!

Attention all chicken farmers! Take a look at our

READY-PLUCKED CLUCKERS

THE CHICKENS THAT ARE BRED TO BE BALD!

GROW!

No more messy, time-consuming plucking! And get this... because these "fowl-looking" birds don't have to waste energy growing feathers, they'll get big quicker!

READY-PLUCKED CLUCKERS
BALD IS BEAUTIFUL!

Weird, eh?

Zak

40

I knew he had something gross up his sleeve – those poor chickens! (But then I would say that 'cos I'm a veggie and proud of it!)

The next day we received another email from Joe. But it wasn't about animal problems.

To: Zak
From: Joe

Hi Zak

Just received a weird email for Mr McMisery on Aunt Meg's computer. I know we shouldn't have read it but we had no idea it was for him.

It said,

Why no B.G. report?
Everything OK?
Contact immediately!

What's a B.G. report? Is it some sort of a test done on sick animals?

Joe

PS We sent a reply, explaining that Duncan's in hospital, but the computer couldn't send it.

No idea why – something wrong with their email address, I imagine.

PPS Alice says thanks for the "Pony Pal" info.

We showed Joe's message to Dad.

"Never heard of a 'B.G. report'," he said. "But it's nothing to do with animals. I should suggest they let Duncan sort it out when he's better. And I haven't got a clue why they can't send a message back. Any ideas, Zak?"

But this was one boffiny question he couldn't answer.

"Not sure," he said, "but I'll look into it."

I didn't think it mattered at the time. The B.G. report was probably just something to do with Duncan McDougal's work. Perhaps he still had business connections in the horse-racing world. He was probably on a committee or something. Yeah, that would be it. At least that's what I thought...

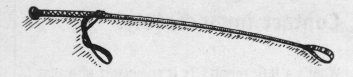

Paddocks and Padlocks

We called Dad in to have a look at Auntie Jackie's new advert.

"I think it's great," he said. "But I hope she doesn't mind that drawing of her!"

My French isn't good and I've never done Latin but...

I DO SPEAK FLUENT "PONY"!

Understanding the language of ponies means I can sort out badly behaved animals quietly and without fuss. Call me to discuss your needs (in English not Pony!)

"I've told her it's up and running," Zak said. "She's really pleased and said she'd be sending Alice's stuff over to us, later."

When the pony info came I could see that it was just what we wanted. Or just what Alice wanted, anyway. I had a quick read and forwarded it on.

To: Doug, Beth and Zak

Hello, you three!

What a jolly nice advertisement! I'm absolutely delighted with it!

I was very interested to hear about your client, Alice Appleyard. The situation you described is all too common, I'm afraid. I come across so many ponies like Lotty. It's boredom, of course, but there's plenty Alice can do. I've attached a file on the subject...

KNOW YOUR PONY!

Jackie Canter's information files

DEALING WITH A BORED PONY

What would happen if you were locked in your bedroom for months and months with nobody to talk to and nothing to do? You'd go potty!

And this is what can happen to a pony that spends his life alone in a stable. Ponies are sociable animals that

enjoy being with their own kind and need plenty of space to graze and exercise.

When ponies get bored they start to behave strangely. These are the signs to look out for...

Weaving

The pony moves his head from side to side for long periods of time. He might also lift first one front leg and then the other in a repetitive manner.

Box walking

Another repetitive habit that some bored ponies adopt is to walk around the stable in circles as if in a trance.

Crib-biting

Chewing the top of the stable door is a common symptom of boredom in ponies.

Wind-sucking

Crib-biting can sometimes develop into wind-sucking. Having gripped the stable door with his teeth, the pony will suck air into his stomach. This can cause digestive problems and sometimes even worse illnesses!

Door-kicking

This is another symptom of boredom. Apart from damaging the stable door, a pony can damage himself and upset other ponies in the stable, too!

THE SOLUTION

There are anti-chew fluids to paint on stable doors, metal grills designed to stop weaving, rubber mats to protect kicked doors and toys to keep ponies amused. But a bored pony needs more than this to live a happy, healthy life!

The best solution is simple. A bored pony needs the company of another pony, or, if this isn't possible, lots of love and attention from his owner. Put him outside as much as possible so he can exercise and watch the world around him, and perhaps most important of all, ride your pony as often as you can!

Wish Alice luck, and if there's anything else I can do, let me know.

Love and best wishes

Auntie Jackie xx

PS I was so impressed with Beth's drawings that it's given me an idea! I've always wanted to produce a "Pony Language Poster" – something that could be pinned up in stables or given to clients. Would Beth be interested? I'd pay, of course! And you might like to put it on your website, too. Do let me know if you're interested!

Wow, I'd have done it for nothing! But I must admit the mention of money made me email back even quicker with a definite "YES!"

A short while later, Auntie Jackie sent me some photo references with the relevant text underneath. To be honest, it *did* look a bit dull. But that's where my illustrations would help and I was determined to produce a masterpiece!

I started straight away and it wasn't long before I was totally wrapped up in it.

While I was working my thoughts turned to Alice. Was she managing to make friends with Lotty? Would the pony respond to the advice we'd sent? Would Alice ever manage to ride her? My thoughts were interrupted. Dad was calling upstairs. Something about a flipping (or was it a flapping?) chicken.

"Hold her for me, would you?" Dad asked as I walked into the surgery.

Betty Bantam (Bantams are a small breed of chicken) squawked as I lifted her out of the box.

The problem with Betty was that she'd been causing havoc in a neighbour's vegetable patch. She'd been flapping up onto the fence and fluttering down into the forbidden garden.

The answer was to clip her wings. Sounds cruel, doesn't it? But it only meant that Dad needed to trim a few of her wing feathers. Betty wouldn't feel a thing.

The job didn't take Dad long but it would quickly put a stop to her lettuce-munching sessions.

Things were still tricky for Dad and I could see that he needed me in the surgery. The poster artwork would have to wait.

Some time later, after helping to sort out a flea-ridden cat, a choking dog, an injured gerbil and a poorly lizard, I slumped down in the office for a cup of tea and a choccy biccy.

There were a few emails, and one was from Alice Appleyard. She'd hardly had time to read Auntie Jackie's stuff so I was curious to find out why she'd mailed me.

To: Beth
From: Alice

Hi Beth

Thanks for the pony stuff – that's going to be *really* helpful!

I'm staying in Suzy's old room (Aunt Meg's daughter who used to own Lotty) and this morning I decided to have a look through a box of her old pony things. There were photos, rosettes, books, magazines and a scrapbook about Lotty.

The scrapbook's filled me in on Lotty's past. Suzy and her pony have won loads of things: gymkhana games and even some jumping competitions. She describes Lotty as a friendly, laid-back sort of pony who loves to be ridden. They both look so happy in the photos, it's no wonder Lotty was going mad being shut in all day.

I'm determined to get her back to the way she was before Suzy left home. It's *so* exciting! And I've discovered something else, too. I think it must have been a history project, or something. It's really good! In the project, Suzy says that the horse has been one of the most important animals in the history of the world! Take a look at this...

HORSES IN HISTORY

The world might be a different place if we hadn't learned how to tame and ride horses! These days, horses and ponies are usually kept for sport or pleasure, but just look at some of the jobs they've been used for in the past...

Helping humans to travel long distances

Making daily deliveries

MILK

Helping with the heavy work on farms

And guess what? Suzy says that Lotty's descended from the sort of ponies that were used in the coal mines. Can you imagine Lotty doing that sort of work? I reckon that would be enough to make any pony go mad. Do you know anything about pit ponies? Were they badly treated? I'm intrigued!

Best wishes

Alice

Dad came into the office.

"Sit down," I said, "and read this email while I make you a cuppa."

I got up from the computer and offered him my seat.

"Thanks, Betts," he said, peering at the screen. "Now, what's all this about?"

I put the kettle on and left him to have a read.

"Know anything about pit ponies, then?" I asked, five minutes later.

"Only that they were forced to work underground in the coal mines. It must have been a miserable life for them."

Ponies underground? This was news to me.

"They must have been desperate to get back to their fields in the evening."

Dad raised his eyebrows. "You must be kidding! The miners couldn't bring them to the surface every day. The ponies spent most of their lives underground."

"That's terrible!" I said.

"Yes, it was terrible," Dad replied. "And it wasn't exactly a picnic for the men who worked with them, either."

Wow! Never mind Alice, I was keen to find out more about this for myself!

"Got any info I can read, Dad?"

I could tell from his grin that he'd had one of his good ideas.

"Even better," he said, "I know somebody who actually worked with pit ponies."

This was sounding promising.

"You know old Bob Blatherwick with Thumper the border collie? Well, he worked down the mines in the 1930s as a lad. Go and see him, he'll tell you all about it."

Later that day, I scrolled down our client list and found Bob Blatherwick's details. He's a bit deaf so when I phoned I don't think he quite understood why I wanted to interview him. Still, I arranged to call round the next day. I could explain everything when I got there.

Zak asked if he could tag along.

"Sure," I said. "You can be my secretary and take notes."

"Thanks!" he scoffed. "What did your last slave die of?"

But a plan was starting to form in my mind.

"We could do a special feature on the pit ponies that Bob worked with," I suggested. "Call it *The Underground Ponies*, or something."

He wasn't totally sold on the idea. "Aren't you working on something for Auntie Jackie?" he asked.

"Yes, and it's almost finished. Now do you want to do this or not?"

"Yes, OK, keep your hair on!" he said. "Let's see what Bob's got to say first. It might not be as fascinating as we think."

The next morning, before setting off for Bob's, we had another email from Alice. Life on the Isle of Jigg was far from dull, it seemed…

Hello Beth

It's been hectic here! Wait until you hear about our latest disaster...

I've been spending loads of time in the stables with Lotty, and Joe suggested that we took her out for a stroll on the lead rope. It seemed like a good idea – sort of the next stage in her progress, I guess. So we led her outside and ... she went bonkers! She was rearing up and squealing – I couldn't hold her. Even worse, Joe hadn't quite finished mending the paddock fence so Lotty galloped through a gap and disappeared across Jigg. Disaster!

There are high cliffs all around the island coastline and I had a nightmare vision of Lotty galloping over the edge.
Then Joe came to the rescue. While I stood there panicking, he fetched our bikes and told me to get on and start pedalling!

We cycled for hours, arriving at the top of a high cliff on the far side of the island. There was no sign of Lotty. We looked down at the rolling waves 200 feet below, dreading what we might see. Thankfully, there was nothing but rocks and a few gulls bobbing about on the  waves. The coastline dropped down to a small beach and an old croft (a sort of little cottage) nestled into the hillside. We decided to see if anybody was at home. Perhaps they had spotted our missing pony.

Imagine our disappointment when, nearing the croft, we realized that it was ramshackle and empty. Walking down the path we could see that most of the windows had fallen out.

Then, through one of the gaps, we noticed something moving. I threw down my bike and ran to the window. It was Lotty! We'd found her! Honestly, Beth, I was *so* pleased to see her. And *she* seemed pleased to see us! I think the excitement of escaping her stable had exhausted her. She seemed ready to go home and let me take her rein without any fuss.

So there we were with two bikes and a pony. It would have been a right pain if we'd had to leave a bike and come back for it later. In the end, Joe managed to walk along sandwiched between the bikes, holding them by the saddles while I walked ahead with Lotty. It took ages!

Still, I'm pleased to say that our little adventure has made me even more determined to win Lotty over. I must admit, I can't wait to ride her. So I'm continuing to follow your Auntie's advice, but I'm not going to rush things.

Joe's been great. He should finish fixing the paddock fence this afternoon. Aunt Meg had bought all the materials – we found everything stacked behind the hay barn. Mr McMisery just hadn't bothered to do anything with it! Not much of a handyman, was he?

Anyway, there's one last thing to tell you about. Yesterday, we were walking Lotty past the field with the forbidden barn when something odd happened. She stopped dead in her tracks. Then, standing still, she pricked up her ears, flared her nostrils and snorted. What does that mean? She seemed to be concentrating very hard, almost as if she was listening to something in the barn.

But what could be in there? Joe and I couldn't hear anything. Anyway, it's padlocked; the last person to go inside would have been Duncan. Weird, isn't it?

We plan to turn Lotty out in the paddock tomorrow. I'm sure she'll improve when she's able to spend all day in the fresh air. I hope so!

Best wishes

Alice

And here's a message from Joe to Zak...

Hi Zak

Just to let you know, apart from the runaway pony, all the other animals are doing fine.

Joe

PS More smelly news ... it's Alice! She comes in from the stables each evening and, PHWOAR! The smell's incredible!

It was almost time to set off for Bob's but I had something else to do first. Auntie Jackie's Pony Language Poster was ready. I sent one copy to her and another to Alice.

Now she could look up things like pricked ears, flared nostrils or any other pony expressions and know exactly what they meant!

From: Beth

Hi Alice

Thanks for your last email. I'm glad it all turned out OK and that you're still making progress with Lotty. Take a look at this cartoon strip I've just done for my Auntie Jackie, you might find it interesting.

Keep in touch

Beth

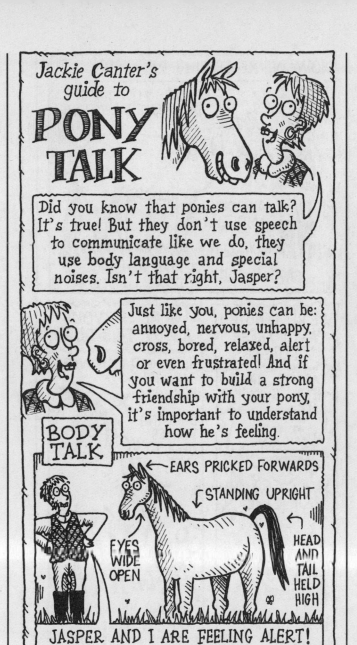

THE SPECIAL NOISES

On the way to Bob's, Zak and I chatted about Alice's email. Was there really anything going on in the barn? Could Lotty hear something or was it a smell that was spooking her – rat poison, maybe?

"Maybe they should take a quick look inside," Zak suggested.

But I didn't think it was a good idea.

"They'd need a good reason for breaking in," I said. "That Duncan McThingy would do his nut if he found they'd ignored his warning."

I didn't realize at the time how right I was...

It's the Pits!

There was no stopping old Bob Blatherwick once he'd started reminiscing about his days in the coal mines. It was lucky we'd borrowed Dad's tape recorder, Zak couldn't have written fast enough! Hearing about Bob's work with the pit ponies was fascinating. Years of labouring underground had left him fragile and deaf. But there was clearly nothing wrong with his memory as he described the dirty, dangerous life of a miner and his pit pony.

When the interview was over, I offered to make a cup of tea while Zak stroked Thumper and Bob searched for an old diary and some photos.

As we left his house, I looked back to see Bob Blatherwick standing in the doorway with Thumper at his feet.

Old memories had been stirred. No doubt his thoughts continued long after we'd left.

Although we'd got loads of info, the visit had been sort of sad, too. I think Zak felt the same way and we agreed that the life of a pit pony was a story worth telling.

But I didn't feel sad for long. The next email from Alice cheered me up.

HELP!

From: Alice

Hello Beth

Had to tell you; we released Lotty into her newly fenced paddock yesterday. It was a bit scary, actually. She became very excited and galloped around, kicking out and whinnying loudly. We thought she might jump the new fence and gallop off across the island again.

But she soon calmed down and today, when I put her out, she just seemed relaxed and happy to be outside.

I might try her with the bridle later. She needs to get used to being tacked up again. And if all goes well, I'll put the saddle on her tomorrow. (I've been working really hard, cleaning her tack!)

Just think, I could be riding her in a few days. I'm *so* excited!

Alice

"Alice is getting really attached to that pony!" I said. "She's going to be *so* gutted when it's time to go home."

Zak shrugged his shoulders. "Nothing we can do about that."

Maybe not, but the holidays wouldn't last for ever and … hmmm. An idea suddenly came to me. And it was an especially good one, so, leaving a puzzled Zak by the computer, I rushed upstairs to jot down some notes. I'd keep this project to myself for a while – until I'd finished *The Underground Ponies* story, anyway.

The Underground Ponies story soon started to take shape. Dad helped with the text but left the artwork to me. The drawings were tricky. Any artist will tell you that horses' legs are a nightmare! I usually draw them standing in long grass but that's a bit difficult when they're supposed to be down a coal mine.

After a few days, it was Zak's turn to do his technical bits. Goodness knows how he gets things to appear on our website. To be honest, I don't really want to know. I can just imagine his boring, boffiny explanation!

Zak seemed to have found a mate in Joe Appleyard. But it wasn't an interest in computers they shared, more a fascination with anything yukky or smelly. They seemed keen to keep the topic going, anyway...

From: Joe

Hi Zak

If you think your bald chicken ad was freaky, listen to this!

There was a messy and incredibly smelly

incident today while I was milking the cow.
Everything was going well – the milk was
squirting into the bucket and Decibelle was
munching some hay.

Then she decided to produce a cowpat.
Nothing unusual in that, except that this
time, the old girl coughed whilst still doing
her business. I was caught in a sort of "poo
explosion". Not nice, as you might imagine.

Still, none of it went in the milk!

Alice tried to ride Lotty today and fell off.
She'd been doing fine until she kicked Lotty
on to go a little faster. But she kicked too

hard and the pony took off at full pelt,
leaving Alice on the ground behind her.
I don't think Alice wanted to tell Beth about
it. I guess she's a bit embarrassed.

That's all for now. I'll let you know if there's
any other smelly news!

Joe

Of course I was bound to find out about Alice falling off and Joe knew it. I wouldn't let on, though. Instead, I'd let her be the first to read *The Underground Ponies* story. I'd based it on the diaries that Bob Blatherwick had lent me. He'd written them over 70 years ago when he first started working in the mines.

Back through history, horses and ponies have done loads of different types of work, but Blackie the pit pony must have had one of the hardest jobs of all...

From: Beth

Hi Alice

Hope it's all going well with Lotty. Thought you might be interested to know that we've put some info about pit ponies on our website. It's called...

The Underground Ponies

THE STORY OF BOB BLATHERWICK AND HIS PIT PONY, BLACKIE

12th January 1932

My name's Bob Blatherwick, I'm just 15 and I finished school today! Grand, eh? At last I'll be able to work in the mines with my dad.

I'll be working with a pit pony. Dad says there's plenty of new ones being trained all the time. Only the best are picked, mind, ones that'll settle down to wearing a harness, pulling heavy weights and such like.

15th January 1932

My first day underground. Another lad, called Wilf, showed me the ropes and introduced me to my pony. He's called Blackie and when I saw him he'd just had a haircut!

WILF

Wilf explained how tails and manes would get dirty and tangled in the mines so they give them a proper old trim before putting them to work.

Blackie's job is to pull the heavy trucks (called drams) and Wilf spent the day explaining the commands I'm to give my pony. Orders like, GO TO LEFT! and COME BACK!

a dram

16th January 1932

Our first full day's work and I'm done in. I'll bet Blackie is, too!

I couldn't wait to leave school, but sitting in a clean, warm, dry classroom don't seem so bad, now. I'll bet Blackie would like to be back in the fresh air, too. But at least I can go home each night. Pit ponies spend most of their lives in underground stables.

Our job is to take full drams from the coalface (where the miners dig the coal) and pull them to the pit shaft where the coal can be lifted to the surface.

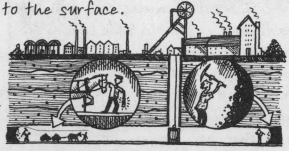

I have to admit to liking my little pony. Blackie's gentle and affectionate and he likes to give me a right good nuzzle when I scratch his head!

19th January 1932

The end of our first week. By heck, I've never felt so tired. Earlier today, my lamp went out and we had to find our way to the pit shaft in the dark. I were quaking in me boots. Darkness in the mines is blacker than black with not the tiniest glimmer of light to travel by. I thought we might lose our way, but my brave pony remembered the route and led us through the narrow tunnels to the shaft. Good lad, Blackie! I was so relieved that I gave him a bit of my snap (food).

7th July 1932

Blackie and I have been together for several months now and we make a good team. Mr Thwaite, the old man in charge of the underground stables, is always saying how I'm a "right good pony man". He's called the ostler and I'd like to have his job one day! There was an accident with a runaway dram earlier. An old pony called Blossom suffered a damaged leg and had to be put to sleep. She'd been working down here for years, poor lass. Arthur, Blossom's driver, was right upset. He'd grown fond of her - and even had a tattoo of Blossom's head on his arm. It's a hard life for these pit ponies.

MR THWAITE

14th April 1936

It's a few years since I last wrote
in my diary and much has changed!
Old Mr Thwaite has retired and guess
who got his job? Me! I'm
dead chuffed. So
Blackie has another
driver now but I still get
to look after him and all the other
ponies in our underground stables.

20th June 1936

We've decided to go on strike! We
want more money, more holidays and
safer working conditions and we'll
not do a stroke of work until the
coal mine owners improve our lot.

I've persuaded the other miners that
the ponies should be brought up to
the surface until things have been
sorted.

21st June 1936

I've looked forward to the day when I could see my ponies out in the sunshine and there they are, at last! But poor old Blackie ain't with them. He's got a poorly leg. Eeh, can you credit it? He might have been dirty and tired down the pit but he's never been injured or sick. It's a sorry tale...

Travelling up the shaft lift was a frightening experience. After years in the darkness many of the ponies were getting jumpy as we neared the surface and daylight.

The excited animals were led down a track and into a muddy field. Then chaos broke out! I'm not sure if it were panic, excitement or fear that gripped them but whatever it was, it caused ten minutes of total madness. The animals were bucking, kicking and squealing – going at it hammer and tongs. And that were when Blackie got injured. I've bandaged his leg as

best I can but I'm not sure if he'll be fit enough to work again.

10th July 1936

I've enjoyed tending to the ponies up top, but the strike is over and we're going back underground in a few days. At least, me and the other ponies will, but not Blackie! I've passed him unfit to work and he'll be sold on in a week or so. Maybe a milkman or a farmer might have some less strenuous work for him. He's worked hard down the mines and can spend his remaining years enjoying some daylight. Not that I'm going soft or nowt, just doing my job, that's all!

Lotty's lucky she wasn't around back then!

Write soon,

Beth

A few days later, Dad arrived back from a hospital appointment. He had a smile on his face – the plaster cast was gone.

"I won't be passing any more work over to old Smuggins," he said. "Now I've got two arms, I intend to get my business back on the road!"

He was certainly in a good mood.

"Who's due in this afternoon then, Betts?" he asked.

It seemed a shame to pour cold water over Dad's enthusiasm but I had to tell him.

"Sorry, but I'm afraid it's … old Mrs Ferris and Honey."

The colour drained from Dad's face and his smile faded with it.

"Oh no, please. Not those two!" he whimpered.

So what was the big deal about this particular customer? I'll tell you.

Honey is an old Golden Retriever. An old, *incontinent* Golden Retriever! And if you're not sure what *incontinent* means, well, let's say … the reason babies wear nappies is because until they learn to use a potty, they're incontinent. Get the picture?

Honey was very old and Mrs Ferris couldn't face the truth.

"Oh no, Mr Kennel, I don't mind a bit. I'll keep clearing up Honey's little messes until she's better."

But Honey wasn't going to get better. That was the whole point.

"Perhaps you'd be kind enough to take a look at her. She could do with a little clean-up."

Dad looked down at the old dog and sighed, then he jotted something down on a notepad and handed it to me.

While Dad trimmed the smelly, matted fur from Honey's rear end, I went into the office and printed a copy of the advert he'd asked for. Mrs Ferris didn't have a computer but the printout would help Dad explain his idea.

"Honey's had a good life, Mrs Ferris. Her troubles are a sign of old age and as I've said before, there isn't a cure for this problem. However, I do have one last suggestion."

Mrs Ferris's eyes lit up. "Yes, Mr Kennel, what do you suggest?"

Dad continued. "Pants, Mrs Ferris!"

The old woman's eyes grew even larger. "Did you say pants, Mr Kennel?"

"Yes, incontinence pants for dogs. They're an American invention. You might consider ordering a pack. Beth's printed out some information for you."

INTERNET VET ADVERTISEMENTS

PURCHASE PET PRODUCTS FROM AROUND THE WORLD!

Incontinent old dog?
Constantly clearing up smelly messes?
Feeling "BROWNED OFF"?

Fit the old mutt with a pair of

POOCHY-POO PANTS

They come in a variety of attractive styles.

Order today and remember:
IF A JOB'S WORTH DOING IT'S WORTH DOING IN A PAIR OF
POOCHY-POO PANTS!

SPLURP!

Mrs Ferris squinted at the sheet of paper. "Oh dear, I don't have my glasses with me. I'll take it home and have a read, Mr Kennel."

"I'll explain if you like..."

"No, no. Don't worry, I'll have a good read later." Dad looked relieved.

"Yes, OK, Mrs Ferris. Let me know what you decide."

I waited until they'd gone before speaking.

"Don't remind Zak about that ad, Dad, it's just the sort of thing he and Joe seem to find funny."

"Well it's not funny for Mrs Ferris and Honey," Dad said. "I don't look forward to their visits but I do sympathize with the old lady. She loves that dog and can't bear to think of life without her."

Dad was out at a farm for the rest of the day, so after he'd packed his stuff and driven off I checked the email. Just as I hoped, there was another instalment of the Potty Lotty Trotter story.

From: Alice

HELP!

Hello Beth

At last I've managed to ride Lotty!

She's calmed down loads since being in the paddock all day. I've slowly got her used to being tacked up with her bridle and saddle, and I've been walking her round the smallholding every day.

So the big moment arrived at last. I was really
nervous about getting in the saddle and I
think she could sense it. I wasn't going to tell
you, but I'd actually tried to ride her a few
days ago and she threw me off! And Lotty was
a bit twitchy when I got in the saddle this
time, too. She reared up, which made me slip
backwards. I was out of the saddle but
hanging on with all my strength.

Joe helped me back up. "Go on!" he
whispered. "You can do it. If you give up now
she'll think she's won."

Joe was right. I tried to remember what I'd
learned on my pony-trekking holiday last
summer: be firm but gentle and let the pony
know who's in charge. Lotty seemed to read
my body language. When I sat up straight and
tightened the reins to gain control she
responded well and after a few wobbles we
were riding around the paddock.

That was a few days ago. Since then I've been riding *every* day. Lotty's a different pony now she's being ridden – I love her! She's quiet and patient and sort of perfect, really!

But even *more* interesting, listen to this...

This afternoon, Lotty started acting funny again. It was in the same place – the field with the forbidden barn. And this time, Joe and I heard something, too. It sounded like somebody hitting a door with a big wooden mallet.

It was rather spooky so we didn't hang around. Anyway, the weather was looking stormy and I was keen to get Lotty back to her stable.

But guess what? We're going back with a torch and crowbar later. We're sure there's something in there and we're going to investigate!

Wish us luck!

Alice

PS There's been another email for Duncan:

SEND B.G. UPDATE OR THERE'LL BE TROUBLE!

What can we do? We don't know who's sending them!

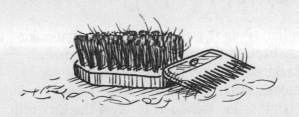

Identity Crisis

My imagination was working overtime as I waited to hear back from the Isle of Jigg. What *was* in the barn? Did the mystery emails have something to do with it? Zak reckoned that the emailers must have cancelled their email address after sending each message. That way it would be impossible to trace them. And Duncan McDougal must have his own secret way of contacting them. What was he up to?

Before Dad got back another email arrived.

To: Beth and Zak
From: Alice

You'll never believe what we've found, it's incredible!

Earlier, while it was still light, we made our way back to the barn when the storm was breaking. The rain stung our faces as we trudged through the mud. After a few attempts, Joe managed to lever the lock off. It was dark inside and there was a strong

---

smell (and it wasn't rat poison!). I switched on my torch and we crept inside. The torchlight jerked nervously around on wooden beams and bales of straw. Then suddenly it lit up two red spots. A pair of eyes! We both gasped.

Keeping my torch on the eyes, we moved closer and soon realized it was ... A HUGE HORSE!

Using the crowbar, Joe opened some of the windows that Duncan had boarded up. This was no ordinary horse – it had incredibly long legs. In fact it was the most magnificent-looking animal we'd ever seen. But he didn't look happy. His head hung low, and his ribs were showing. A self-filling trough had provided water but the poor thing looked tired and weak. Any food or hay had been eaten long ago.

Barney (we've been calling him that because we found him in a barn!) was reluctant to leave his prison, but after some friendly encouragement we managed to lead him outside. Flashes of your emails were running through my head as we made our way back to the farmhouse: "act with confidence!", "be gentle but firm!", "give him lots of pats and strokes!".

It was such a relief when we finally got back to the stables and out of the rain.

Once we were inside we set to work. Barney had become quite mucky lying on his dirty bedding and the rain had actually done a good job of cleaning him! So Joe dried him off while I prepared some food. It must have been his first meal for quite a while, the poor thing.

Mum was flabbergasted when she saw Barney. She's sure Duncan McDougal is up to no good so she's driven into town to report our discovery to Sergeant McDuff, the island police officer.

Why would Duncan keep such a fantastic horse locked in a barn?

We'll keep you posted.

Alice

Amazing, wasn't it? But what about Lotty? Had the pony and horse met each other yet? Dad still wasn't back so I had a look through his books to see if there was anything useful I could pass on to Alice. The way she described Barney made him sound like a very special sort of horse. A class above your average pit pony, anyway!

From: Beth

Hi Alice

Has Barney met Lotty yet?

I've been looking through Dad's horsey books and they say that female horses tend to be the leaders in a group. So although she'll be much smaller than Barney, she might try to boss him around. I wouldn't take any risks, anyway, so don't let them get too close.

Dad's out at the moment but I'll put him in the picture when he gets back.

Take care

Beth x

Within half an hour I had a reply.

From: Alice

Thanks for that, Beth.

We've got Barney dried off and fed now and put him in the other stable next to Lotty's. The dividing wall reaches to their shoulders so they can see each other without causing any trouble!

But what a noise there was when they first met. A lot of squealing and ears going back, but it didn't last for long. More excitement  than anything else, I reckon. I've left Joe with them now, but guess what happened while I was leaving? Leaning over the stable wall, Lotty reached up and started grooming Barney's mane with her teeth! So sweet! I suppose they've both been lonely without another horse for company. They certainly seem to like each other anyway.

Let us know what your dad says.

Alice x

PS It's really blowing a gale outside.

When Dad finally got back he was surprised and worried when he heard the news.

"A horse? Locked in the barn? For several days? Good Lord!" he said. "But they shouldn't be stuffing him with food; it could make him ill!"

"But he was hungry, Dad. Why shouldn't they be feeding him?" I asked.

Dad was shaking his head as he sat down at the computer. "If he hasn't eaten for a few days, large amounts of food could give him an illness called colic. I'd better email them immediately!"

But looking down at the screen we saw that there was already an email from Alice, waiting to be opened.

To: The Internet Vet
From: Alice and Joe

Please help us, Beth! Is your dad back yet? Barney seems sick. He's got swollen patches on his body and he's stamping the ground. He seemed OK when we found him, just weak and hungry. What's gone wrong?

Alice and Joe

PS Mum's not back yet.

"Blast!" Dad said. "Just as I feared! They must get a vet to look at Barney."

Zak and I looked at each other. Dad seemed to have forgotten why Alice and Joe had contacted him in the first place.

"There isn't a vet on the island," I said.

Zak joined in. "And surely the sea will be too rough for anybody to cross over from the mainland. What can we do?"

Dad looked up from the computer screen. I could tell that things were serious.

"Right! I've seen a lot of colic cases and things can sometimes turn nasty. Even a minor attack can last for hours. It might be a long night. This is what we'll do. Zak, phone round and cancel all appointments for this evening's surgery. I don't want any interruptions while I'm dealing with this. Betts, make us all a cup of tea and some sandwiches. I'll email some advice to Alice and Joe and we'll see if we can sort this situation out."

So off we went, leaving Dad to tap out his message.

THE INTERNET VET

Hello Alice and Joe

Now listen carefully. I know you've been doing your best to help Barney but he shouldn't have eaten large amounts of food so soon after you found him. This is what's made him ill. He almost certainly has an illness called colic, which is like a very bad stomachache. Barney really needs an injection, but without a vet we'll just have to hope that it's not too bad an attack. The stomachache will be quite painful, so stay with him – and watch to see if he has a poo. This might sound a bit odd but once he's pooed he'll feel a lot better.

Make sure he's got a deep bed of straw to lie on.

Mail me back as soon as you can and let me know how it's going.

Good luck

Doug Kennel

It was ten o'clock in the evening when the next email came through.

From: Joe

(HELP!)

Doug

He seems worse. I think the pain must be bad because he's started rolling around. We've put down plenty of straw to cushion him but we can't calm him down. When he  stops rolling he just stares at his stomach. Is there anything else we can do?

Alice is staying in the stable with Barney and I'm going to be here on the computer so we can keep in touch. Mum's still not back.

Joe

PS Another disaster! Sergeant McDuff just phoned to say that the road's blocked and Mum can't get back to us. The storm's blown several trees over.

PPS Barney hasn't pooed yet.

Dad replied immediately.

Hi Joe

You're doing your best so try not to worry.
Barney might get some relief from being
walked round, but be careful, he's a big horse
and you don't want to get squashed!

He really does need to poo. Making a horse
nervous or excited can sometimes work.
Leading them into a horse-box is one method:
they get excited if they think they're going on
a journey. But I'm not even sure if you've got
a box and with a horse of that size it would
be too dangerous to try it, especially in a
howling gale. I'll contact you if I can think of
another way.

I'm sitting at my computer so keep in touch.

Doug

Time dragged by. Zak and I stared at the blank
screen while Dad read his newspaper.

Suddenly, Dad stood up, staring at his paper in
disbelief.

"Jumpin' jellyfish!" he shrieked. "Blue Gin!"

Was the stress getting to him? Had he finally
flipped his lid? Thankfully, no. All became clear when
the newspaper article was spread out on the table.

Daily Press

MULTI-MILLION-POUND RACEHORSE KIDNAPPED!

Blue Gin, three-time winner of the Cheltenham Gold Cup, has been stolen from his stables in the village of Trussocks. Police say that a large ransom demand has been made.

If you have any information about the stolen horse, please contact the police immediately.

He has the distinguishing mark of three swirls of hair on his forehead. Police warn that Blue Gin's kidnappers could be armed and

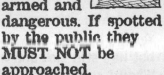

dangerous. If spotted by the public they **MUST NOT** be approached.

Perhaps we wouldn't wait for Alice and Joe to mail us with an update after all!

THE INTERNET VET

To: Alice and Joe

Hope Barney's doing OK.

In fact, we think we know what his *real* name is! A racehorse has been kidnapped over on the mainland. Look very carefully at Barney's forehead. Are there three swirls of hair? If so, we think he's really Blue Gin and the police must be informed *immediately*.

Go and check. QUICK!

Beth and Zak

Wow, this was getting really exciting! But the horse was still very ill and Dad wasn't going to be happy until the colic had gone.

It didn't take long for Joe to reply.

From: Joe **HELP!**

Yes, he has the three swirls,
but he's still sick and hasn't pooed yet.
When I called Mum on her mobile, she was
still stuck with Sergeant McDuff. I explained
about Barney being a kidnapped racehorse but
Sergeant McDuff says we'll have to sit tight.

They can't send a police boat over to the island until the weather improves. We're not bothered about that, we just want Barney to pull through.

Joe

I tried to imagine the scene at the smallholding with the rain lashing down on the stables and Alice inside, trying to help the sick horse through his illness.

"Doesn't sound too good," Dad said. "Either way, we'll know by morning."

It was a long night. Zak and I tried to stay awake but some time in the early hours we nodded off. Dad continued to keep in touch with Joe, offering advice and encouragement until the sun came up.

I'd fallen asleep in an awkward position and woke with a stiff neck. Looking around I saw that Zak was still out for the count and Dad was over by the kettle making a drink. He looked over.

"Fancy a cuppa?"

"Please. How is he, Dad. Have you heard?"

He walked over with two steaming mugs.

"It looks like …" Dad smiled and passed me the tea, "… he's going to pull through. I had a message from Joe about five minutes ago. He said the storm had caused a short power cut and the stables were plunged into darkness. The racehorse was terrified; Joe thinks Blue Gin must have thought he was back in the locked-up barn. Then in the darkness, Joe smelt the thing he'd been waiting for all night. And when the lights came back on, his suspicions were confirmed … the sick horse had pooed! Blue Gin soon improved after that."

I hadn't felt that happy for ages. Blue Gin was going to be OK and we'd helped to save him.

"Zak, Zak, wake up. Blue Gin's going to be OK!"

It took him a moment to recover from the violent shaking. "Huh? What … I … er … he's … OK? … Excellent!"

So there we were, feeling pleased with ourselves and thinking that everything had worked out brilliantly…

Heroes!

We were still chatting about Blue Gin when another email came through.

From: Alice

Something's happened. Another email's arrived for Duncan McDougal. Must be from his kidnapper friends. They're angry that he hasn't kept in contact and ... THEY'RE COMING TO GET BLUE GIN!

Mum's had to spend the night in town. The roads are still blocked and we're scared. The kidnappers must be on the island – they might turn up at any minute!

We want to get away and hide until the police come, but there's a problem. Blue Gin refuses to leave the stables. He won't budge.

What can we do? PLEASE GET BACK TO US QUICKLY!

Zak and I looked nervously at Dad. We were hundreds of miles from the smallholding – how could we persuade a sick horse to leave his warm stable and go out into a howling gale?

"Well, there is something they could try," Dad said, already tapping out a reply. "It's a bit of a long shot, but it's the best I can think of."

THE INTERNET VET

From: Doug

Hi Joe and Alice

If Lotty's been grooming Blue Gin, it sounds like they've bonded well and also that Lotty's acting as the leader. Put their head collars on and lead Lotty outside first. Hopefully, Blue Gin will follow her.

Doug

PS Put Lotty's saddle on, too. You might need to ride her.

Five minutes passed before a reply came back.

From: Alice

It worked! Setting off across island right away. Joe says we might be able to hide at Calum's cottage (postman who gave us fertile eggs). We've phoned Sergeant McDuff and he said that Mum's set off to reach us on foot as the roads are still blocked. Explained we couldn't wait. So the sergeant said he'd try to meet us at Calum's if the route was clear. Left note for Mum on kitchen table.

Alice

Wow! It was the sort of thing that you see in films except that this was *really* happening. But what more could we do? Dad had done his best as a vet and, from what Alice had said, the police on Jigg were up to date with the situation.

"I hope they're OK," Dad said. "I suppose we might not find out for days."

But for once, Dad was wrong. Four hours after Alice's email, a message arrived from Joe.

From: Joe

HELP!

Made it to Calum's cottage.
Using his computer. No sign of Sergeant
McDuff. Storm has passed and we've managed
to dry off and eat something but there's a
problem. Two, actually. Calum's worried that
the kidnappers might have seen the message
we left for Mum. If so, they could turn up
here. There *is* somewhere else we can hide but
Blue Gin's hurt his foot and is hobbling badly.
Any ideas?

Joe

Dad was on to it immediately.

Hi Joe

Take a close look at Blue Gin's feet. You may
need to wash them off. Let me know what you
find. He might have cut himself or have a
loose shoe.

Doug

The reply came back in minutes.

Hi Doug

Once we'd washed the mud off we saw Blue Gin had a sharp stone trapped in his hoof. Calum's managed to get it out with a screwdriver. Reckon Blue Gin's OK to walk further now. Must go, think kidnappers coming!

Joe

And that was the last we heard from them. For a few days, anyway. It was frustrating not being able to help and horrible not knowing what was going on. We had to be patient. And while we waited for news, we chatted about Lotty Trotter and Blue Gin.

"You were right about one thing," Dad said. "Blue Gin *is* a special sort of horse. Racehorses are thoroughbreds, intelligent but highly-strung too."

"Highly-strung?"

"Yes, a bit nervy and jumpy," he said. "You need to know what you're doing with horses like that, they spook easily."

"But what about Alice and Joe?" I asked. "They don't know anything about thoroughbreds!"

Zak cut in. "I wouldn't worry," he said. "Blue Gin doesn't sound like he's in any state to cause trouble."

Dad sighed. "Sadly, I think you're right. Oh dear, I feel like I should be doing something more to help!"

But there was nothing more we could do. Finally, after three days, we heard from them. And when you hear what happened, I think you'll agree that they did well to get back to us that quickly!

To: The Internet Vet
From: Alice and Joe Appleyard

HELP!

Dear Beth, Zak and Doug

You must have been wondering what happened to us after we left Calum's cottage. Well, now that we've recovered, we can tell you...

Once Calum had picked the stone from Blue Gin's hoof, we led the horses to the abandoned croft. Do you remember? It's the place where we found Lotty when she escaped from the paddock.

The storm had passed by now but we were cold and very, *very* tired. We had no idea how long it would be before help came. Then we heard the sound of a car. We thought it must  be Mum and the police ... but it was the kidnappers! How had they found us? We were sure Calum wouldn't have told them where we were.

We discovered later that, minutes after we'd left Calum's cottage, the kidnappers had pulled up in a four-wheel-drive. (The blocked roads hadn't stopped them from finding us!) They threatened Calum with a gun and if it wasn't for one of them discovering hoof-prints in the mud, I dread to think what might have happened. Anyway, the criminals sped off, following the trail that led straight to our hiding place.

Seeing their car skid to a halt outside the croft, we grabbed the horses and ran as fast as we could down a track to the sandy cove. We were trapped and the three kidnappers were running towards us. As they got closer we could see that the nearest one had a scar across his face and ... a gun! The one behind him was fat with a big bushy beard and the last one was small and bald! They were a terrifying sight.

I've never, *ever* been so frightened! But Joe was brave. Still holding Blue Gin, he stepped forward to shield me and Lotty from the villains. It was no use. Beardy grabbed Blue Gin and pushed Joe over into the water. Joe scrambled over to where I was standing with Lotty. Scarface raised his gun. Was this it? Was he *really* going to shoot us?

Then we heard a strange noise overhead. A police helicopter! A voice blasted out through a loudspeaker:

THIS IS THE POLICE! GIVE YOURSELVES UP, YOU ARE SURROUNDED!

And they weren't joking! Two high-powered boats appeared with armed police jumping into the water and wading onto the beach.

Beardy dropped Blue Gin's rein and together with Baldy he ran off across the sand. But Scarface wasn't going anywhere without a fight. He raised his gun AND FIRED!

It hit Lotty – I heard the bullet thud as it went in. The sound of gunfire spooked Blue Gin who was standing with his back to Scarface. He kicked out, knocking Scarface flat on his face, and then he galloped off.

By this time Joe had taken Lotty from me. It took all his strength to hang on to her. She was terrified and in pain and the noisy helicopters were spooking her. I tried to calm her, stroking her neck and making reassuring noises. Eventually she calmed down enough for Joe to check her over. You could still see the whites of her eyes, though. "Where did it hit her?" he said. "How could he do that? All right Lotty, all right..."

Nearby, police had handcuffed Scarface and were leading him to some police cars that had just arrived. Looking across the beach I could see that Baldy and Beardy had also been caught...

"The saddle!" Joe said. "Look, the bullet hit the saddle! Just here, Alice!" I leaned over to examine the small hole that Joe was pointing to.

"It didn't go through!" he said, lifting the saddle to check underneath. "The leather protected her!"

And he was right. The bullet had hit the thick padded bit of the saddle and stuck there.

"Joe! Alice! Over here!" We looked up to see Mum and Sergeant McDuff running across the sand towards us.

Sergeant McDuff took Lotty's reins. Mum hugged us both. I looked over to the sergeant. "Where's Blue Gin?" I asked.

"He's fine, dear. D'nay worry. Look over there!" And there he was, away in the distance being led along by a policewoman. Then we saw another figure, running past the racehorse and towards us. It wasn't long before we realized who it was. An exhausted postman!

After the kidnappers had left, Calum had phoned the police and told them exactly where we were. Then he'd run all the way down to the croft to see if he could help. Good old Calum!

The kidnappers are being held in custody on the mainland. Mr McMisery is still too ill to be questioned but they'll arrest him soon.

Blue Gin and Lotty are fine. A police vet has checked them over. She says Blue Gin will need to stay on the island while he regains his strength but he'll be transported home as soon as poss.

Oh yes, and take a look at this newspaper cutting. We all hit the headlines in the *Daily Press* yesterday!

Daily Press

BLUE GIN RESCUED!

Heroes Alice Appleyard and her brother Joe are both recovering at home today after saving a stolen racehorse from a gang of ruthless kidnappers.

RUTHLESS KIDNAPPERS

Police have revealed that the multi-million-pound thoroughbred Blue Gin is alive and well after his kidnapping experience. *For full story see page 3.*

DOUG KENNEL

Alice and Joe say they would like to put it on record that without help from Doug Kennel, The Internet Vet, things might have turned out differently. "I don't think we would have made it without him," say the Appleyards. "He offered us veterinary help and friendly encouragement throughout the whole ordeal. His dedication to his work is fantastic and we'd like to say a big THANK YOU!" And another big THANK YOU goes to brave postman Calum Bartlett, who risked life and limb to save the children from the brutal kidnappers.

CALUM BARTLETT

What a story! We'd had some exciting times running The Internet Vet website but this topped everything.

Dad was grinning from ear to ear. "Some good publicity, at last. And in an important newspaper, too!"

"Let's hope Matt Smuggins sees it," Zak said. "I bet he's never saved the life of such a valuable animal."

Of course I was just as pleased as Dad and Zak that everything had worked out but I had work to do. My secret project was almost done, so I nipped upstairs to finish it.

A few days later, we heard that Alice and Joe's Aunt Meg had arrived home.

From: Alice

HELP!

Hi Doug, Beth and Zak

Just one last email to say thanks and goodbye. Aunt Meg's back and we're travelling home tomorrow. Honestly, her face was a picture when she heard about our amazing adventure!

I'm going to miss dear Lotty *so* much. But Aunt Meg says I can visit again next summer so at least I've got that to look forward to.

Joe says, "Hello!" Remember our broody hen and the eggs Calum gave us? They've just hatched and guess what? They're ducklings – not chicks! OK, Calum, nice joke, I guess we've still got a lot to learn about animals!

Thanks again for everything

Love Alice x

"That's that, then," Dad said, leaning over to switch the computer off.

"Hang on!" I said. "Take a look at this. I knew Alice would be sad to leave Lotty, so I've designed something for her to print out and take home."

I took the mouse from Dad and clicked on my folder.

PONY RIDING FOR THE PENNILESS!

FIVE WICKED WAYS TO WANGLE FREE RIDES

IT REALLY WORKS!

1 If there's somebody in your class who owns a pony ... make them your best friend. Buy them birthday presents, laugh at their jokes, give them your sweets, offer to do their homework — be so nice to them that they'll be forced to say...

GRIN!

YOU'RE SUCH A GOOD FRIEND — WOULD YOU LIKE TO RIDE MY PONY?

2 Help out at your local riding school! Whether it's raining, snowing, or blowing a gale, turn up with a smile on your face and: brush the ponies, muck out the stables, paint the jumps and clean the tack. Make yourself so useful they'll have no choice but to say...

NOD!

THANKS FOR ALL YOUR HELP. WOULD YOU LIKE A FREE RIDE?

3 Find somebody who's too busy to exercise their pony. Many pony owners can only find time to look after their animals at weekends. If you're an experienced rider, offer to ride their pony during the week! You might also need to volunteer for other jobs in order to win them over. Stuff like: clearing up horse poo from the fields and polishing their riding boots. They'll be delighted, saying...

TA!

FANTASTIC! HERE'S THE KEY TO THE TACK ROOM. RIDE HIM WHENEVER YOU LIKE!

4 Offer to look after somebody's pony while they're on holiday or away for the weekend. Once they know they can trust you, they'll be overjoyed to have found a reliable animal lover who'll clean, feed and ride their pony while they're away. Honest! They're bound to say...

> WOW, I WAS HOPING TO FIND SOMEBODY LIKE YOU. I'M VISITING MY GRAN THIS WEEKEND — DO YOU FANCY LOOKING AFTER MY PONY AND HAVING A FREE RIDE?

> EXCELLENT!

If all else fails you can make a...

5 VIRTUAL-REALITY PONY-RIDING MACHINE

All you need is:

a rocking-horse

a peg

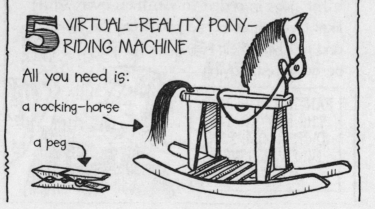

a tape recorder

two coconuts for recording "clip-clop" sounds on the tape recorder

a fan

wellies

some pictures of the countryside (cut from magazines)

cycle helmet with cardboard peak taped on

a metal coat-hanger

CLIP-CLOP!

The
End

THE INTERNET VET

WIN PRIZES

WHY NOT VISIT OUR WEBSITE?

We're at:

WWW.INTERNET-VET.CO.UK

PET STUFF — Stacks of fascinating facts and other PET STUFF

WIN STUFF — Take part in our competitions and WIN STUFF!

BOOK STUFF — the latest info on forthcoming titles

LINK STUFF — Check out other pet sites on the LINK STUFF page

THE INTERNET VET

Also in this series:

Help!
My dog can't stop farting

Help!
Something's eaten my hamster

Help!
My cat's too fat

HORRIBLE SCIENCE

**Also illustrated
by Tony De Saulles**

Ugly Bugs
Blood, Bones and Body Bits
Nasty Nature
Chemical Chaos
Fatal Forces
Sounds Dreadful
Evolve or Die
Vicious Veg
Disgusting Digestion
Bulging Brains
Frightening Light
Shocking Electricity
Deadly Diseases
Microscopic Monsters
Killer Energy
Suffering Scientists
Explosive Experiments
The Awfully Big Quiz Book
The Body Owner's Handbook
The Terrible Truth About Time